Fire Mag

Fire M

MW00967312

Mark Jeffrey Stefik

Illustrated by Mark & Barbara Stefik

The Oberlanders: Book 6

The Oberlanders

Published by Portola Publishing
Portola Valley, Ca. 94028 USA

© 2020 by Mark Jeffrey Stefik

All rights reserved under International and Pan-American Copyright Conventions. No part of this book may be reproduced in any form by any electronic or mechanical process (including photocopying, recording, or information storage and retrieval) without permission in writing from the publisher.

Illustrations for the book are by Mark Jeffrey Stefik and Barbara Stefik.

This book is a work of fiction. The characters, incidents, and dialogue are drawn from the author's imagination and are not to be construed as real. Any resemblance to actual events or persons, living or dead, is entirely coincidental.

Fire Magic the sixth book in *The Oberlanders*. The books describe fictional events in a universe including the planets Sol #3 and Zorcon.

Further information about the series can be found at www.PortolaPublishing.com

Library of Congress Cataloging-in-Publication Data
Copyright Office Registration Number: TXu 2xxxxxxxx
Stefik, Mark Jeffrey
    Fire Magic / Mark Jeffrey Stefik
Edition 7
ISBN: 978-1-943176-16-8

Cinderwan had just begun her Elder training in the Earth Element when a voice in the fireplace flames spoke to her. The Fire Ancient was calling her to come to where the sky meets the sea. The Phoenix offered to accompany her on the journey. He neglected to mention that he planned to jump into a volcano with her. Or that she would need to reclaim her own voice. Only then could she begin to understand her higher purpose.

Books in *The Oberlanders*

Magic with Side Effects (#1)

Magic Misspoken (#2)

Old Magic Awakens (#3)

Magic Reprogrammed (#4)

Earth Magic (#5)

Fire Magic (#6)

Water Magic (#7)

Air Magic (#8)

Space and Time Magic (#9)

The Sendroids series continues after *The Oberlanders*. Information about both series can be found on the website www.PortolaPublishing.com

ACKNOWLEDGMENTS

Special thanks to Charley Thweatt. His songs of hope lift the hearts of many people. Somehow, he inspired Charley, the awakened Cookie Machine.

Thank you to our wonderful friends and early readers who read earlier versions of the folktales of *The Oberlanders* as we developed them. Special thanks to Asli Aydin, Phil Berghausen, Eric and Emma Bier, Danny Bobrow, J.J. and Stu Card, Nilesh and Laura Doctor, Ollie Eggiman, Lance Good, Craig Heberer, Chris Kavert, Ray and Lois Kuntz, Raj and Zoe Minhas, Ranjeeta Prakash, Mary Ann Puppo, Jamie Richard, Lynne Russell, Mali Sarpangal, Jackie Shek, Morgan Stefik, Sebastian Steiger, Frank Torres, Paige Turner, Blanca Vargas, Barry and Joyce Vissell, Alan and Pam Wu, Meili Xu, and their kids and young relatives.

Thank you also to the people of Gimmelwald and Mürren, Switzerland in the Swiss Alps and the people of Vetan in Valle d'Aosta in the Italian Alps. These places inspired us with their natural beauty and stillness, and the power of the mountains, lakes, forests, and waterfalls. The people of the Alps have histories and traditions that reach back into legend and folktale.

Fire Magic

CONTENTS

Fire Magic

"We were the strangest aliens on Sol #3, but there were others from quite much farther away living in Cinderella's back yard." *From Sol #3 Expedition Review AB99A, Marie GottMothercus, Zorcon University Archives.*

Fire Magic

1 The Scholar

Officially, the Scholar was the Keeper of Books, Maps and Records for the Kingdom of Oberland.

Unofficially, he was a holder of wisdom, a discoverer of secrets, and an advisor to elves, dragons, bears and other students who lived and studied at Oberland School.

The Scholar's Tower was at Oberland School.

Oberland School had been a sanctuary for Cinderella in her student days. The school was not only an escape from her duties as a kitchen maid. It was her door to a larger world.

At Oberland School, the Scholar was a guide to new worlds of knowledge and wonder. For Cinderella, the Scholar was first a teacher and then an advisor. He encouraged her to find herself and exercise her abilities. His belief in her countered the disdain of her stepmother and the drudgery at home.

After she became queen, Cinderella continued to consult the Scholar as a trusted advisor on important matters.

One time the Scholar had teased her, reminding Cinderella that she was no longer a student at Oberland School. In mock protest, she told him, "The 'Advisor' position is a lifetime appointment!"

This morning Cinderella was puzzled by a single question:

Who was Pele?

King Jorgan and Queen Cinderella walked to the Scholar's Tower. There was a bell by the tower door. Cinderella rang the bell and waited for the Scholar.

Cinderella rang the bell and waited for the Scholar.

From inside the tower Cinderella heard the first sister bell reverberating. The ceilings and hallways focused the bell's ring. Deeper in the tower a third bell began to vibrate, carrying the sound deeper into the Scholar's home. Cinderella heard the shuffle of sandals on the stone floor inside the tower.

A man's voice called out, "I'm coming! I'm coming!"

The doorknob turned and the tower door opened.

A peculiar red-haired man wearing green and brown clothes and sandals stood before her. Half glasses perched on his nose. Although he looked young, his red hair was streaked in grey. An open book rested in his hands.

The Scholar gazed up at Cinderella. He brightened as he recognized her.

"Your Majesty!" he said, straightening up. "Perfectly in time for Morning Tea."

King Jorgan stepped into view from around the tower.

"Your Majesties," corrected the Scholar, shifting to the plural.

A red-haired man dressed in green and brown stood before her.

"There are morning buns enough for us all. Welcome! Welcome! Please come in."

The smell of fresh baked morning buns and cinnamon tea filled the air. King Jorgan smiled, and Queen Cinderella beamed.

2 Fire Bird

 spiral stairway rose Inside the Scholar's Tower. Shelves with books lined the stairway. The tower was a vertical library.

"A spiral stairway lined with books rose inside the tower.

Every few feet there was a window and a seat, where a reader could sit to read and take notes.

The Scholar led them to a dining area by the kitchen. A table was set for four. A tall bird entered the dining area, wearing an apron. It carried silverware in its claws and set four places at the table.

Cinderella recognized the bird as the Phoenix. She had seen it a few times over the years. The students said that the Phoenix was the Scholar's pet. They were friendly to it but did not pay it much attention.

Cinderella said, "Hello, Phoenix."

The bird bowed to them briefly. It squawked as it walked.

"I know," said the Scholar to the bird. "That will happen pretty soon now, in a matter of weeks."

The bird squawked some more.

"Maybe the Queen can help," said the Scholar looking at the Queen. "I will ask."

The big bird chirped.

"I won't forget," said the Scholar.

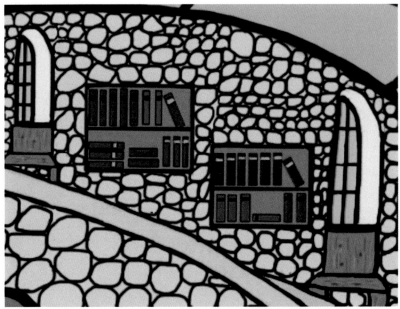

Every few feet there was a window and a seat.

Jorgan and Cinderella looked at the bird and the Scholar. In its clicks and whistles the Phoenix appeared to be carrying on a conversation and making requests of the Scholar. It was curious.

"Is there a way that we can be of help?" asked Cinderella.

"First things first," said the Scholar bowing. "Everything in its proper time."

"We must find out what your Majesties seek," he said, glancing to the bird. "But other protocol comes before that. There is the immediate matter of morning buns and cinnamon tea."

"I am pleased to see you again," said Cinderella to the Phoenix. "We will help you if we can."

The Phoenix squawked slightly and bowed.

The Scholar nodded to the big bird. The Phoenix went back to the kitchen and brought out a lovely plate of morning buns. Cinderella said, "Thank you," to the bird as it placed the morning buns on the table.

"Thank you," said the Scholar.

"And, of course, cinnamon tea." The Scholar poured aromatic cups of the steaming tea. "Shall we be seated?" he asked.

Cinderella sat down. Then the King and the Scholar sat, and the big bird perched on a stool.

They sat and they settled. They munched and they sipped. They sighed and they smiled.

After a while, the Scholar asked, "Now, your Majesties. How may I help you?"

The Phoenix brought out a plate of morning buns.

Cinderella began. "I seek knowledge," she hesitated. "It may be nothing. It was part of a dream."

At that moment the Phoenix started squawking and chirping at the Scholar. The Scholar nodded and turned to Cinderella. Cinderwan smiled.

"We all sleep," began the Scholar. "And we all dream. What matters is not whether something is a dream, but whether we are paying attention."

Cinderwan nodded and continued, "There was singing."

"Perhaps you could sing it to me," suggested the Scholar.

Cinderella remembered the face singing in the flames of her fireplace. "I have many blessings," she said, "but singing is not one of them." She cleared her throat and began to recite the poem.

> The way of the Fire
> Is bright and hot.
> The walk is outside
> The journey is not.

The Phoenix squawked and fussed.

The Scholar's eyes opened wide. He sang the next verse of the ballad.

> Go to the island
> Where the sky meets the sea
> To walk by the side
> Of the Ancient Pele.

Cinderella was startled. "You know this song?" she asked.

The Scholar replied. "There are many verses to the Fire Ballad."

He looked at her and continued. "Synchronicity is the universe's way of saying that you are on the right path. The Phoenix and I were talking about Pele before you knocked."

Cinderella was startled.

The Scholar continued. "My Queen, I do not need to search my library for this information."

Cinderella was baffled.

The Scholar explained, "Pele is an Ancient manifesting the Fire Element. She usually resides at a volcano."

"I have never heard of her," said Cinderella.

"Pele lives on the other side of the world," continued the Scholar. "She is creating an island called Hawaii."

"Why were you talking about Pele?" asked Cinderella looking to the Phoenix.

"The Phoenix is a fire bird. He lives for a thousand years. Then he must burn on a pyre to renew himself. He must make his pyre at a volcano. Soon."

Cinderella nodded and began to understand.

"A new Phoenix will rise from the ashes. Our Phoenix is number 999. The next Phoenix will be number zero. It is almost time for 999 to make his pyre."

"Oh, my," said Cinderella looking at the bird. Then turning to the Scholar, she asked, "So if he is number 999, then has this been going on for 1000 millennia?" concluded Cinderella.

"Much longer," said the Scholar. "The numbers start at zero again after each thousand. There have been phoenixes since the beginning. On each cycle the phoenix makes its pyre on an active volcano to renew itself."

"999 requests to go with you," he added.

The bird squawked again and ran to Cinderella. 999 looked into her eyes and put its head on her lap. In her mind, she heard it say, "Thank you."

3 Students Arrive

ama Bear knocked and entered through the courtyard door. She bowed and greeted the King and Queen saying, "Your Majesties."

"Good morning, Scholar," she continued. "Niner," she added, nodding to the Phoenix.

Mama Bear greeted everyone.

To the Scholar, she said, "I heard my name as I came up the path. Also, a familiar ballad."

The Scholar nodded. "Her Majesty brought me the Fire Ballad this morning. She asks about Pele."

Mama Bear turned to Cinderella and bowed. She then asked, "If I may

9

ask, Your Majesty? How did the ballad come to you?"

Cinderella described how her own face appeared in the fire, singing the ballad.

"I came here this morning to ask the Scholar about Pele. As you know," she paused, "I cannot sing. I recited a stanza, and he sang more of it."

"And the time for Niner's pyre approaches," added the Scholar.

"And many dragons and other students will arrive this morning," added Mama Bear, "and others will soon depart for Amerland."

Cinderella's face had appeared in the fire.

"This is no coincidence," suggested King Jorgan, noticing so many related events happening at once.

"I feel that I am being swept along by events that I don't begin to understand!" exclaimed Cinderella.

Mama Bear smiled at her and patted her hand.

"Sometimes a journey opens for us. Taking it mindfully is the best that we can do," she said. "The journey will take us to places that we need to go."

Mama Bear continued. "As several of you know, I am a Fire Elder."

To Cinderella, she said. "Your Majesty, the ballad calls to you. You are invited by Pele to train as a Fire Elder. This is an important invitation. Very few are invited. There are many challenges for those who train, and they find that their responsibilities will touch many lives."

Cinderella was still. She looked around the room and then to Mama Bear. "I am just beginning to learn about all these things, Mama Bear. Deep training in more than one Element is unusual for Elders, right? Are there other such Elders, or more Elders in my kingdom?"

"That is difficult to answer precisely," said Mama Bear. "There are usually ten of us, two for each of the elements. Elders are introduced to all of the elements, but each Elder is trained deeply in one element. An Elder is trained in the Element closest to its nature."

She continued, "To answer your unasked question, I don't know why you are being trained in this way. Training an Elder deeply in multiple elements is rare."

Suddenly the Phoenix chirped. The Scholar shook his head but said nothing.

"You have started your training in the Earth Element," Mama Bear said, "which is about equanimity and perceiving what endures. The Fire Element is about creation and destruction. It brings great energy and great responsibility."

Mama Bear turned to the Scholar. "The Scholar is an Associate," she said without explaining further. She then looked at the Phoenix. "The line of the Phoenix is *very* old. The Phoenix predates the Elders. You will be able to speak with Niner as your Elder powers grow. Then you can hear his tale directly."

Cinderella nodded.

Mama Bear waited a moment. She turned to King Jorgan. "The timing is good for travel. We should talk with the dragons," she said. "The students are about to arrive."

Just then a chatter of voices, clicks, and squeaks could be heard in the courtyard. There was knocking at the back door. Immediately, knocking sounds echoed around the house.

"Good morning, Scholar!" sang voices from the back door.

The Scholar rose from his chair.

"Your Majesties, the students and the young dragons are here. Please excuse me for a moment," said the Scholar. The Scholar, the Phoenix, and Mama Bear walked to the courtyard door.

A squeal of delight came in from the courtyard. The Royals heard the Scholar's heralding voice as he greeted the new arrivals. "Zoe! Sparky!"

The students were excited, "Mama Bear! Scholar! Phoenix – you are here today!"

Cinderella turned to Jorgan and said, "I had completely forgotten that the bi-mester starts today! Let's join them."

Mama Bear's voice could be heard above the fray. "Of course, I will have strawberry and cinnamon pie for everyone!"

"Zoe! Sparky!"

King Jorgan and Queen Cinderella arrived at the back door and stepped out into the chaos of the courtyard. The arriving human and dragon students had been away for six months of schooling in the dragon kingdom of Amerland. Another group of students and dragons was streaming out of the school and dormitories. They would travel to the dragon kingdom for their next six months of schooling and wilderness training.

Years before, King Jorgan had been a student in the exchange program. He spent alternate bi-mesters training in his Father's kingdom and training in the dragon kingdom. His grandfather, Jorgan the First, had started the exchange tradition after an adventure in his youth began an alliance between Oberland and Amerland.

In the center of the courtyard Chloe and Zoe were talking with friends. Dragons circled in the sky, preparing to land in the courtyard. Each had a human rider or a package on their back. Little puffs of flame and smoke came out of their mouths when they exerted themselves.

At the entrance to the courtyard more kids and grownups from the kingdom were arriving. Grown elves and young people came from Elf Village. Grown bears and cubs were arriving from the bear village. Grownups and kids were arriving from the Noble houses. Red Riding Hood and Sage were in the courtyard.

Sage went to inspect one of the egg wagons as it was pulled around the edge of the courtyard. It was heading toward the Bell Tower and the student complex beyond. Something was odd about the wagon. No child or dragon was pulling it. Something red was harnessed to the wagon. Cinderwan looked carefully. A giant red ladybug pulled the dragon egg wagon. The ladybug was the size of a large dog. It pulled the wagon slowly and carefully.

At that moment, Red Riding Hood spotted Jorgan and Cinderella at the door and shouted, "The King and Queen!"

King Jorgan and Queen Cinderella waved to everyone and Jorgan said, "Welcome! Welcome!"

Everyone came to the courtyard to meet the arriving students.

Cinderella spoke next. "It is wonderful to see you all again. We want to hear what has happened in school in Amerland during the bi-mester and we will share with you all what has been happening here in Oberland."

She and Jorgan looked to each other, thinking about recent events surrounding the Fairy Godmother and Charley. Jorgan raised an eyebrow and turned back to the students.

He spoke, "We will have the welcoming dinner tonight in the castle. Students should wear their dress robes – including first-time students – except for the eggs."

There was a chorus of giggles about eggs wearing robes, and then everyone in the courtyard started talking and greeting again. The welcoming dinner was a tradition. It was repeated every six months when students were exchanged for the next bi-mester.

Cinderella and Jorgan greeted everyone. They spoke briefly with the arriving and departing teachers. The Scholar announced that the Council Room in the Scholar's Residence was nearly ready for a gathering of teachers. The Phoenix headed back to the kitchen with Mama Bear to make sure that the tea and cinnamon buns would be ready.

A giant ladybug was pulling the dragon egg wagon.

With all of her attention on Elder training and the upcoming trip to Pele, Cinderella had forgotten that it was the beginning of a bi-mester. It didn't seem to matter. Her journey was racing to parts unknown, but life in Oberland Kingdom would continue. Everyone was busy. Perhaps at this time she was not needed very much in the kingdom.

4 Morning Buns and Tea

Cinderella and the Scholar looked out the windows of the Council Room to check on the arrival of the teachers. The room was ready for the meeting. The Phoenix had set the table and laid out fresh morning buns and tea.

Every time the Council Room door opened, the scent of morning buns and cinnamon tea wafted out to the courtyard.

Cinderwan and the Scholar looked out from the Council Room.

The Council Room was used as a study hall when Oberland School was in session. It had a large round table and was connected to the Scholar's Residence and his tower library.

A group of teachers came into the Council Room from the courtyard. Mama Bear and Gabby led the way. Gabby was Hansel and Gretel's mom. She was the departing master for Science and Pragmatics. Departing masters like Gabby would leave in a few days to teach in Amerland, the dragon kingdom. Two dragons and Elfin John followed behind them. Elfin John was returning home from Amerland. He taught Debate and Readings.

He would continue those classes in Oberland during the next bi-mester.

Dragons love cinnamon. Mama Bear opened the door and the aroma of cinnamon wafted into the courtyard. The dragons smiled in anticipation of the treat.

King Jorgan and Queen Cinderella greeted the teachers as they entered the Council Room. The informal council gatherings were for renewing friendships and sharing important news before the formal dinner with the students. By tradition, the gatherings had no formal program. They settled around the Council Room table. Refreshments were served.

Gabby chatted with Dorix, the dragon-lady teacher. Dorix was master in Debate and Readings. This was her second tour to Oberland. Dorix knew her way around.

Master Danix's voice boomed, "These Council Room chairs will soon be outdated! The new student designs from the last bi-mester Maker Competition prove to be much more comfortable for us dragons. They have "Wing Rests," and are now being copied all across Amerland!"

Master Danix's voice boomed.

Elfin John also spoke excitedly. "We brought two dragon eggs with us on this trip!" Dragon lore said that dragon eggs hatched in Oberland grew up to be dragons of great wisdom and leadership. The students in the Dragon Hall would raise the hatchlings, with help from everyone. King Jorgan and Queen Cinderella beamed at the news.

"A question for you all," began Dorix. "Seers in our kingdom have been talking about a fluctuation in the field. They reported that an asteroid has moved outside of its normal orbit in the asteroid belt. People also heard mountains echoing the word 'Yameru'. What do you know of such omens here in Oberland?"

Mama Bear looked to Cinderella, who cleared her throat. Although Cinderella knew that the echoes from the mountains came from Papa Bear's Halting Word magic, such information was Elder business rather than school business.

"Some of you know the Fairy Godmother," Cinderella said, looking around the room. Everyone nodded. "Sometimes her Good Deeds and magical activities have unexpected side effects."

There were a few chuckles around the table, as people anticipated a story. Cinderella described the cookie disaster briefly. She did not elaborate on Papa Bear's role.

"He is made mostly of titanium."

She continued, "A side-effect of the Fairy Godmother's misadventure and magic was that a new and very unusual person was created. He has joined our community. Everyone calls him 'Charley'. He is neither an elf nor a noble nor a bear nor a dragon nor a Phoenix." She said this with a little bow to the Phoenix, who was still in the room, serving morning buns.

She left out the part about how Charley had apparently been changed and awakened by Elder Coyote. That, too, was Elder business.

Cinderella continued, "He is grown. In many ways he is brilliant, and he learns quickly. And yet he seems to have the mind of a child. Oh – and he is made mostly of titanium."

Immediately there was a chorus of exclamations.

"How amazing!"

"How could that be?"

Mama Bear picked up the conversation and steered it for the teachers. "One of the questions we are pondering is 'How should we raise him?'"

Danix boomed in, "Is there only one of his kind? I dare say that Dorix is the only one of her kind – always answering questions with more questions! Should Charley be in the House of Sky or House of Land?"

The House of Sky and the House of Land were the two houses in which the exchange students were organized each bi-mester.

There was laugher around the table about the student house rivalry. Many of the teachers noticeably relaxed at the attitude that Cinderella and others had about Charley. Mama Bear realized that someone, probably King Jorgan, had already briefed Danix and asked him to help steer the conversation away from Charley's origins.

Jorgan added, "All of the children will want to meet him and spend time with him."

"Where did the giant Ladybugs come from?"

Mama Bear continued, "And there may be virtue in having him go to Amerland in the following bi-mester." This suggestion reassured the dragons further about the man of titanium, who they did not yet know.

Many heads nodded around the table at the wisdom of the suggestion.

Gabby raised another thought. "And Charley is not the only new being joining us recently. Where did the giant Ladybugs come from?"

Dorix answered her quickly with a debate-style question. "Oh, where did *any* of our peoples come from?" She continued, "We have found that they can greatly reduce the work of the tending and rocking of dragon eggs and hatchings!" Her debating point headed off any discussion about the origins of the Ladybugs. It showed that the dragons trusted the Ladybugs even to care for their new hatchlings.

Mama Bear realized that Cinderella probably had a short royal discussion with Gabby on the Ladybug topic already. Questions about origins were delicate in both kingdoms.

The exchange program was intended to socialize and deepen relationships between the kingdoms. In addition to teaching, the teachers were informal ambassadors. Care was taken to maintain trust and to share information. Diplomatic conversations about official kingdom business would take place at other meetings.

"Our beautiful. Kingdom is just a small part of everything."

The conversation turned to other topics. After a while, King Jorgan rose and addressed everyone. "The Queen and I look forward to seeing you all at the Master's Table in the Great Hall tonight. We have a few things to check.

We hope you find that your apartments are well prepared. Please see Mr. Treebear if you have any needs. He will be our Head Host in the coming bi-mester."

The teachers gave their thanks and sipped their tea, and after a while, left to check out their cottages.

Cinderella turned to Jorgan as they walked back to the castle. "We take comfort in our rituals, don't we?" she asked.

Jorgan nodded. "Long ago, there was much suspicion and little cooperation among the peoples – the humans, elves, bears, and dragons. These rituals strengthen our sense of belonging together."

"Things are changing around us. The Elders expect that something is coming," speculated Cinderella.

Jorgan nodded. "That's what I think, too. Do they know what it is? What do they need you to do?"

Cinderella shrugged, "Our beautiful kingdom is a small part of the world and beyond. Where did the Fairy Godmother come from? What exactly is our little tin man? What is the asteroid business all about?"

Jorgan reflected. "Charley is something quite new for us," he said. Then he added, "Our rituals give us comfort. They may help us to stand together whatever might come."

Jorgan patted Cinderella's hand.

Cinderella worried. "I hope that my Elder training does not pull us apart."

Jorgan nodded and they held hands as they walked back to the castle.

5 Interruption at the Feast

t was always crowded at the start of the bi-mester. The returning and new students had arrived, and the departing students had not yet left. The beds in the dormitories had trundle beds beneath them that could be pulled out – so there were plenty of places to sleep.

There was the usual commotion as everyone entered the Hall.

The departing students packed their belongings for their upcoming trip and prepared the trundle beds for themselves. This made the arriving students feel welcome. A similar pattern would be repeated six months later.

The older students oriented the younger students in the House of Sky and the House of Land. Students in the House of Sky put on their blue robes for the Feast that night. Students from the House of Land put on their red robes.

As the evening approached, the bell in the Bell Tower rang to announce that the hour for the Feast was approaching. The students in their robes headed outside to the paths up to the Great Hall. Elves, bears, dragons, and humans walked and talked in small groups. Teachers walked from their nearby cottages wearing their robes.

The Great Hall was lit for the evening. Everyone anticipated the Feast and the sharing of news. There was the usual commotion as everyone entered the Hall.

The doors were wide open. Tables were set. There were blue tablecloths on the tables for the House of Sky and red tablecloths for the House of Land. Red Riding Hood talked with Gabby as the teachers settled on a raised stage at the far end of the Hall. They talked among themselves and watched the students. Queen Cinderella and King Jorgan were seated in the middle and chatted with everyone.

Red Riding Hood talked with Gabby.

Students gathered and chatted as they entered. Blues went to the left and reds to the right.

Red Riding Hood and Smokey were head proctors for the students. They supervised both houses and were supposed to be impartial in the rivalry between them. Since Red Riding Hood always wore a red robe, some students said that she was partial to the House of Land. Smokey wore his black hooded robe, which some students felt was closer to the blue of the House of Sky. Smokey, however, insisted, that with his nickname, black was the only appropriate color.

The house allegiances of the proctors were a matter of much speculation but little wisdom or real knowledge. There was banter and jest among the students on the topic. The proctors settled the students and then sat down. Red Riding Hood winked at Smokey. Then unexpectedly, she sat down at the blue tables with the House of Sky and Smokey sat down at the red tables with the House of Land. That confused the students who thought they knew the score. A few coins exchanged hands. Bets had been won and lost.

Students gathered and chatted in the Great Hall.

Queen Cinderella and King Jorgan rose and nodded to everyone. Jorgan spoke first. "A very happy welcome to you all," he said, bowing to the teachers and then to the students.

"We have some announcements from our Headmaster before the Feast," he continued. He nodded to Sage.

Sage stepped to the front. Her voice carried to every corner of the room. Wonderful scents of the feast wafted in from the kitchen doors, but everyone focused on Sage.

Sage began. "Classes begin next week and will include both the arriving and departing students."

This was no surprise. School life followed the same pattern every bi-mester.

"Master Gabby and Master Danix will lead classes on Science and Pragmatics. Master James and Master Dorix will lead classes on Debate and Readings."

Sage paused. Then she called out, "Charley!"

Charley stepped in from the kitchen. The lights reflected on his titanium face and arms and his bare feet. His red and blue eyes glowed.

There was a hush across the hall. This was the first time that many of them had seen the "tin man." The story of his appearance had been spreading in the villages since he arrived a few days before. Still, it was amazing to actually see him.

Just then Hansel stood up in his red robe from the House of Land and BC stood up in his blue robe from the House of Sky. Both of them smiled and started to clap for Charley. At once others stood up and began clapping too. Charley's eyes blinked and the teachers rose and clapped. There was a great cheer for the tin man.

Sage spoke again, her voice filling the hall. "We have a robe for you Charley, so that you can join the students in the school. Please come here."

Charley smiled and walked to the platform by Sage. The students held their breaths, wondering whether Charley would join the House of Sky or the House of Land. It was rumored that he had special talents. Whichever house got him would have an advantage in the house competitions.

Sage lifted a robe from the box in front of her. She had made the robe over the last few days, with the approval of the King and Queen. Sage helped Charley into his robe. The robe was in two colors split down the middle. The right side of the robe was blue, matching his blue eye. The left side of the robe was red, matching his red eye.

Sage put the robe on Charley.

Sage started to explain this but before she began there was thunderous roar of approval and clapping from all the students. Charley would belong to both houses. That was a perfect choice! Charley would be welcome across the school. Charley smiled. He was not used to applause. He did not yet completely understand the situation, but somehow it felt good.

Sage went on to explain what was now clear to everyone. "Since there is only one of his kind, Charley will belong to both houses. He will contribute to all of the projects and competitions."

The clapping got louder. There was shuffling as students from both houses stood and cheered. BC in his blue robe and Hansel in his red robe made their way to Charley. The three of them did a high five and cheered "Okey! Dokey! In the Pokey!" Nobody had any idea what that was all about, but it sounded cool. Both houses picked up the cheer and shouted it again.

"Okey! Dokey! In the Pokey!"

The teachers looked to each other in puzzlement. Nobody had any idea where this new cheer came from or where the idea was going.

Sage went back to the teacher's table and King Jorgan got up to speak again.

"We have a few more announcements," he began. Everyone quieted down and he continued. "The rivers are running high from the snow run offs and …"

Before King Jorgan got any farther, the tolling of a bell sounded from the Bell Tower. Two strikes. Then there was a pause. Then there were two more strikes of the bell.

Bell ringing announced the hatching of the dragons.

The door at the back of the Great Hall flew open and the Scholar rushed in.

He raised his hands. Everyone looked to him. The King said, "Yes, Scholar?"

"We have two new hatchlings!" announced the Scholar.

There was another cheer. Jorgan and Cinderella looked to each other and smiled. The eggs had just arrived in the kingdom just in time to hatch. This was a very good omen.

At once, the dragon students from both houses raced to the door to head down to the dragon nursery with Smokey in the lead. The bears from both houses also rushed out the door with BC in the lead. Finally, the elves and humans gathered. Red Riding Hood and Hansel led groups of them up the stairs to the balconies on each side of the hall.

King Jorgan started to say that the students would be temporarily excused, but everyone already knew what to do.

He turned to Cinderella and said, "We will have a celebration at our Feast." The cooks went back into the kitchen to make sure that the Feast would be fine even though it would be delayed.

Cinderella replied to Jorgan, "We need to be flexible. Events move with their own momentum – all of our planning aside."

Jorgan chuckled.

6 Dragons in Wagons

ears in robes entered the Great Hall and set up thunder drums. BC and Papa Bear carried the EarthShaker drum. It was almost too big to fit through the doors of the Great Hall. The bears put the drums on their stands.

Papa Bear eyed the drummers and drums. Beside each drum stood a bear with two heavy drumsticks. They waited for a signal from Papa Bear. Outside there came the sound of wagons and marching feet. Smokey's head came in through the door. He looked to Papa Bear and nodded. Papa Bear looked to him and the drummers. He lifted his drumstick and signaled to the drummers with a nod.

The sound of the drums shook the hall.

At that moment all of the bears struck their drums at once. The sound shook the hall. A chill ran through everyone. The King, Queen, teachers and students all stood. The Welcoming Ceremony for the Hatchlings had begun.

Smokey leaped through the doorway. He roared and breathed a flame up towards the ceiling.

The drumbeats rose to a crescendo. The rhythm made hearts leap. Boom! Boom-boom-tatta-tat-tat-boom-boom-boom.

The dragons entered. They struck the floor with their staffs as they pranced up the aisle. The drumming and pounding shook the Great Hall. The sound grabbed everyone's mind. The dragons danced and paraded to the front of the hall.

Moving slowly alongside the dragons a giant ladybug pulled a wagon carrying the hatchlings.

Suddenly Smokey rattled his stick and the dancing and drumming faded to a whisper. The EarthShaker slowed to a quiet heartbeat. The beat could be felt through the Great Hall.

The dragons pranced up the main aisle of the Great Hall.

Amidst all the commotion and celebration, Cinderwan mused about the times ahead. The exchanges between Oberland and Amerland assured peace. The kingdoms had developed traditions – like the student exchange program and the Dragon Egg celebrations. The dangers of the old wars seemed behind them.

Soft singing wafted down from the balconies. Elfin song touched the hearts of everyone. Cinderella's eyes filled with joyous tears and she reached for Jorgan. He squeezed her hand as they watched the singers. The singing was as moving as the drums. It was as melodic and joyous as the drums were powerful. It was a song of welcome and joy and hope. The procession moved slowly to the front of the hall.

The hatchlings blinked their eyes and looked around in wonder at the hall and the gathering. Dragons surrounded the wagons as the Ladybug pulled them to the King and Queen. Then the dragons stepped back.

Cinderella stepped down from the stage. She bowed by the wagons and blessed the hatchlings. King Jorgan smiled. One dragon hiccupped and blew a little flame. Everyone giggled at the cute hatchlings.

Soft singing filled the Great Hall.

The bears moved their drums to a corner. The singers descended the stairs from the balconies. Two student dragons flew up to the balconies and then walked down with the singers. The students arranged themselves at the tables for their respective houses.

Jorgan stood and spoke briefly. "Our two kingdoms celebrate this happy event. We welcome the new dragons! May there be continued friendship and prosperity and wisdom for us all."

Cinderella also spoke – "and a blessing for our purpose in this great and mysterious universe."

Jorgan nodded, raised his arms and commanded, "Let the Feast begin."

The students whispered to each other.

"This will be great!"

"Save room for Mama Bear's pies!"

Amidst all the commotion and celebration, Cinderwan mused about the times ahead. The exchanges between Oberland and Amerland assured peace. The kingdoms had developed traditions – like the student exchange program and the Dragon Egg celebrations. The dangers of the old wars seemed behind them.

Queen Cinderella blessed the hatchlings.

Charley was a new factor. Would he affect the balance? Were there more like him from wherever he came from and wherever the Fairy Godmother came from?

7 The Maid of the Mist

organ's wings rose and dropped rhythmically. Cinderwan held tightly to the belt around Dorgan's scaly neck. Dorgan was one of the largest dragons. He was carrying her to Hawaii.

Cinderwan held tightly to Dorgan.

They had flown past the coast of Greenland. Now they flew south above a great river towards Niagara. A campground by Niagara Falls was their planned stop for the night. The weather had been smooth, and the winds sped them on their way.

The days since the Feast had been full of preparations. There had been meetings with the teachers and preparations for the bi-mester. The Royal Party would be gone for a couple of weeks. Papa Bear and Sage were watching over the kingdom until they returned.

Hawaii was on the way to Amerland where these students and teachers would resume their studies. After Cinderwan and her party stopped there, the students and all of the dragons would fly further west. Mama Bear had told Cinderwan that there would be another way home from Hawaii, but she had not yet explained what that was. Over the next few days, the travelers would reach the island in the Pacific to pay their respects to a volcano.

Cinderwan wondered what it was like for the Phoenix. Over the past couple of weeks, the Phoenix and the Scholar had been conferring. The Scholar kept a gild-edged book with him and the two of them were studying it and writing in it together.

The travelers descended. They flew over a whirlpool in the river. The roar of Niagara Falls became louder and its mist blew down the river.

They landed and came down on one side of the river. Mama Bear took charge of the students and the rest of the party as they set up camp. Tents were raised. Cooking fires were lit. Everyone was working or stretching from the long journey.

Downstream from the falls there was a short cliff walk. Nodding to Jorgan, Cinderella walked to the edge for a better view of the falls. Jorgan joined her and the two of them climbed down to see the rushing rapids. They sat on a rock to watch the falls. Jorgan was sleepy from the long flight and after a while, he dozed while they sat. Cinderella shivered as mists surrounded them.

"You were expecting, perhaps, a hot shower?" said a voice from the river.

Cinderella knew that voice. "Sage! Whatever are you doing here?" she asked.

Turning towards the voice, she saw the figure of Sage, except that "Sage" was transparent and made entirely of water.

"Oops!" said Sage without thinking. Cinderwan turned to Jorgan. He was completely still, like a statue. The water of the falls was suspended in the air. The ripples on the river were still. Time had stopped.

She turned back to Sage, who smiled at her.

The water figure bowed slightly. "I am not exactly here. Pardon, me. Your Majesty."

Then she bowed and added, "Cinderwan." So, this was Elder business.

"Dear Sage," interrupted Cinderwan. "You seem a little ... liquid. And time around us has stopped. Are you all right? Are the children doing well? Are things fine with Nick?"

The water image flickered for a second. Suddenly Sage shifted. She held a sleeping cap.

"Oh, my," said Sage. "Your instincts are developing well. "Actually, I am sleeping, in a way," said Sage. "Rather, I was dreaming, but I was not entirely lucid. This is embarrassing."

"Now that I am "awake", I see you are by Niagara." The sleeping cap disappeared, and Sage now appeared dressed in her teaching robe.

"This is confusing," offered Cinderwan.

"Indeed," said the watery Sage. "It has been many years since I accidentally projected myself in watery form. Niagara is a power center for the Water Element. In my sleep I was drawn to it."

She continued, "Things are moving very quickly. The veil between waking life and dreaming is less solid than usual."

"This is a projection?" asked Cinderwan, eying the water figure before her.

"Well, yes," continued Sage. "The ability to project comes with Water Magic. But it is best not to do it when you are sleeping, especially when you are not lucid. Apparently, it was becoming urgent to talk with you now, Cinderwan. The Water Ancient nudged me."

"You were expecting, perhaps, a hot shower?"

Cinderwan smiled. "Sage, it is delightful to see you. What is this about?"

Sage composed herself. "Events are developing. I do not have the depth of Elder Coyote to see into the future, and I am not sure which events are important now. You are on your way to see Pele. Your Fire Element training will begin. I see that there will be a healing. All this is good."

"Interesting," said Cinderwan, "but most of this news is not urgent. Is there more?"

"This is a little out of order," continued Sage, "since it is not yet time. Training with the Water Element may come after you finish training in the Fire Element with Pele. Both elements carry great responsibility. Water brings flexibility and quenches fire. I sense that you will be tested."

"I do not understand why this is planned for me," sighed Cinderwan.

"Nor do the rest of the Elders. The Phoenix may understand it. Much is happening," continued Sage. "You remember that Dorix mentioned a disturbance in the Asteroid Belt?"

"Yes," answered Cinderwan tentatively.

"The Fairy Godmother is moving an asteroid. The Elders are not sure what is going on, but Nick tells me that Marie has been visiting the Elf Village at the North Pole. The elves are excited."

"Are you worried for Nick?" asked Cinderwan.

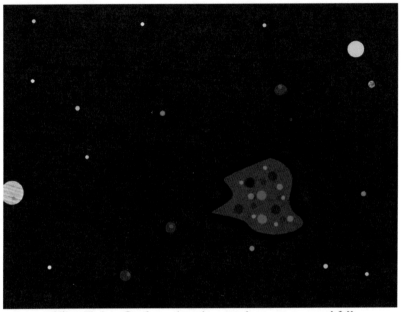

"The Fairy Godmother is moving an asteroid."

Sage shrugged. "All this has a deeper meaning," she said. "It is taught that the training in Five Elements is only done ahead of a great crisis and great opportunity. Earth Magic will help you to maintain awareness in the present moment and in crisis. More is not clear to any of us yet."

"This is *most puzzling*," offered Cinderwan.

"And the Water Element is sometimes most playful," smiled Sage. "Don't take everything seriously!" Suddenly Sage held a platter full of Christmas Faire cookies. She handed it to Cinderwan. As Cinderwan took the platter, the watery cookies became real cookies.

"You pilgrims could use a little sustenance for your travels!" explained Sage.

Cinderwan was pleased. "Thank you!" she exclaimed. "I thought that you had to work for hours to bake your marvelous cookies."

Sage responded, "My dream, my rules! Surprise everyone."

Cinderella nodded. Then Sage turned faced her directly, "Cinderwan."

Cinderella knew that Sage still had something important to convey to her.

"Stay present! And pleasant dreams!" Sage laughed and with that, the water column melted back into the river. The sound of Niagara Falls roared again, and the rapids resumed rushing by.

"My dream, my rules!"

Jorgan woke up. He sniffed and turned to Cinderella. "Something smells good! Where did those cookies come from?"

"A gift from Sage," answered Cinderwan. "Sage's dream world is interacting with the real world. I'll explain later, if I figure it out. Let's get back to camp. The cookies will be a treat for everyone. Then I want to talk with Niner and the Scholar."

The two royals walked back to camp. Sage had wished her 'pleasant dreams.' It was a message, but she did not know what it meant. In the morning, they would fly to Hawaii.

8 Into the Volcano

*S*unrise was hours in the past. Niner and Cinderwan stood above a vast crater. It glowed red and orange. Smoke rose from its depths.

The Phoenix held Cinderella and jumped into volcano.

From their lookout Niner and Cinderwan watched the hot lava. Behind them they heard Jorgan and Mama Bear coming up the trail.

The Phoenix's feathers were red in the glow from the volcano. Cinderwan felt faint from the smoke and sulfur smells. She turned to the Phoenix. His eyes glowed red.

The Phoenix had been quiet for the last part of their climb. During the journey Cinderwan found that she was beginning to understand his squawks and hisses. It was more like telepathy than speech. Niner told her that when he burned, he would shrink down to an egg. When the egg hatched, the Phoenix would need time to regain its memories. The book that the Scholar carried would help him to restore his memories.

The Phoenix's attention was now directed inward as the time approached for his pyre. Cinderwan felt lightheaded when the Phoenix spoke. "Time to go!" he squawked.

Suddenly the bird seized her wrists with its claws. Cinderwan caught her breath as the Phoenix jumped off the edge and then flew with Cinderwan towards the center of the smoky crater. They dropped down into the hot, smoking volcano.

Cinderwan gasped and choked. This was not expected. What was happening?

Tears welled in her eyes. "Jorgan!" she gasped, as they shot down into the crater.

She was going to burn up and die. Her life flashed before her. Back, back, back. She was riding a horse in the pasture with her father for a picnic.

Back, back, back. Her mother was singing to her when she was a little girl. They rocked in a chair.

She cried out, "Jorgan!"

The Phoenix had his rebirth to attend. Why did he take her with him?

Back, back, back.

Cinderella thought about her life as a little girl. Her stepmother and stepsisters had been mean spirited. "Fetch my dress. Fix this ribbon. Mind the stove. Clean the dishes. Brush my teeth!"

How absurd. One time there was a small concert at the house. Her Father was away. "Father!" she cried out.

She remembered a time when her stepsisters sang at a party. Cinderella was not allowed to sing. They said that her voice disturbed everyone. She wore her servant's clothing and served the guests. Then the stepsisters thought it would be amusing for Cinderella to stand in her rags and sing in front of everyone.

She could not remember any songs. She could not remember any words.

Her throat was dry, and her voice cracked. Everyone stared at her and waited.

Her stepsisters laughed. Then other people at the party started laughing too.

The pianist started playing without her. Cinderella cried and ran to her room.

Cinderella could not remember any songs.

After that she never sang again, even when she was alone.

But that was then. This was now.

It was sweltering as they fell deeper into the volcano.

An inner voice spoke to her. "Notice the Stillness within your body and let it still your mind."

Cinderwan focused. Using her Earth Element training, she found her inner refuge. She entered through the door of Stillness. The heat faded.

Thump! Cinderwan had landed. Had she died? She composed herself. She remembered her training with Papa Bear. "Watch your breath. Pay attention." She had stopped breathing. Why breathe smoky air? Her mind cleared.

Wait! The air was not smoky. It was fresh. It smelled of food. It sounded like people at a party. She heard a piano.

Cinderwan opened her eyes.

Fire Magic

9 Cinderwan Sings

*C*inderwan found herself sitting on a piano. Niner was at the keyboard, looking at her. She felt a persistent bass rhythm of the piano. Brum, brum, brum.

Was this real? Was she inside the volcano?

Cinderwan found herself sitting on top of a piano.

It was a large dining room. "People" of various kinds stood at tables throughout the room. Two caterpillar waiters bustled about, carrying drinks.

This was *not* the ballroom of her old family home. These were *not* the diners from that painful party in her childhood. These diners were *not* people she knew.

They were kinds of people that she did not recognize. At one table two diners were green flower people, looking like fairies from a fairy tale. They swayed their heads in rhythm with the music.

A couple with insect-like heads stood at another table. They chatted quietly and looked towards her and the Phoenix. Their black and red eyes flashed in the light. They smiled and nodded.

At another table, the diners had chamois heads. Slim ghostly worms stood at another table.

Torches illuminated the walls, yet the air was fresh.

Where was her pilgrim cloak? Cinderwan had on the blue gown from the Grand Ball.

She missed Jorgan. She almost cried out his name. "Pay attention," she remembered. "Breathe."

The Phoenix kept playing the piano. He lifted his gaze. His eyes glowed. Niner chanted in tones and clicks. His meaning came to her.

> I sing to the earth when I'm praying and kneeling.
> I sing to the rain when I'm cleansing and healing.
> I sing to the sun when I'm planning and forming.
> I sing to the wind when my goal is transforming.
> May we abide
>   in Stillness and Silence and Spaciousness.

The pattern of the verses came to her. Each verse told of an Element.

> I sing to the earth when I'm praying and kneeling. (Earth Element)
> I sing to the rain when I'm cleansing and healing. (Water Element)
> I sing to the sun when I'm planning and forming. (Fire Element)
> I sing to the wind when my goal is transforming. (Air Element)
> May we abide
>   in Stillness and Silence and Spaciousness. (Space and Time Element)

Why was the Phoenix singing to the Five Elements? Was this chant part of a teaching? Was the Phoenix a Master of the Five Elements?

Cinderwan returned to the stillness within. The silence opened and stretched between piano notes. There was stillness in the silence. Her mind entered spaciousness. Cinderwan whispered the ancient teaching to herself, "I take refuge in the Stillness, the Silence, and the Spaciousness." The piano music faded to the distance.

Cinderwan opened her eyes. Everyone was looking at her. They were waiting for her to sing. She thought briefly of her stepsisters laughing as she cried. She could not sing!

Wait. Slow down. That was an old memory. That was then. This is now.

Cinderwan remembered her Earth Magic. "Pay attention. Take refuge in the Stillness, the Silence, and the Spaciousness."

She looked to the Phoenix. He smiled at her. "Snap your finger!" he said.

"I beg your pardon?" she asked.

"Snap your fingers," repeated the Phoenix.

In the Stillness Cinderwan felt joy rising.

For the third time Niner said, "Snap your fingers."

Cinderwan reached out and snapped her fingers. A yellow flame shot up from her thumb. The flame surprised Cinderwan, but Niner had been expecting it. A feather below his beak began to burn.

A yellow flame shot up from her thumb.

"Thank you," said the Phoenix. He kept playing the piano and humming. The flames began to spread over the Phoenix. "Time now to sing," he urged.

Everyone in the room looked to Cinderwan again. She took a breath and sat up. She smiled.

When you sing from your heart
You'll know your part.
When you sing of your mission
Your guides will listen.

Cinderwan's melodic voice filled the room. She was singing! Everyone was nodding and listening. The singing lifted everyone's hearts. She took a breath and sang more.

When you ask what is right
The way shines with light.
Your mission will start
When you sing from your heart.

Tears ran down her face. Everyone watched her in rapt attention, smiling and nodding. The diners all had tears in their eyes and smiles on their faces. Then they stood and they clapped. They clapped for Cinderwan. Everything faded to black.

10 Egg of the Phoenix

inderwan woke up laying on hard ground. She felt Jorgan's arms around her. She opened her eyes.

Jorgan smiled and brushed her hair from her face. "Welcome back," he whispered.

"I was in the volcano. I thought I would die. I sang!" she said, trying to explain everything at once. Looking around, she asked, "Where is everyone? Where is the Phoenix?"

"We let you rest."

"You have been asleep for hours," began Jorgan. "Niner caught you when you fainted by the edge of the cliff. We let you rest."

He nodded his head to a pile of ashes a short distance away on a lava rock.

"You passed out from the smoke," Jorgan continued. "We watched Niner go. He was glorious and happy. This was not his first pyre," he added. "He burned a couple of hours ago."

"Mama Bear and I built Niner's pyre as he requested. He stood there in the flames and sang. The flames burned around him, but nothing happened to him. Suddenly there was a snap and he burst into flames. The heat was extraordinary. The sand on the ground around him glowed like hot lava."

"The Phoenix stood in the flames and sang."

Cinderwan turned to Jorgan. "I had a dream," she said. "Sage told me that I must stay lucid in my dream."

Jorgan nodded.

Cinderwan continued, "I dreamed that I lit the Phoenix on fire."

Jorgan looked thoughtful. "Do you think that your action in your dream ignited the Phoenix?" asked Jorgan.

"So, it seems," responded Cinderwan.

They looked at the ashes of the pyre, now cooled on the ground. Cinderwan got up. She wore her pilgrim cloak again. Her blue gown from the Grand Ball was gone. Mama Bear stepped up and took her arm. "Do not be afraid," she said softly, "Things are more than they seem. Vision is mind."

Cinderwan remembered the verse from her Earth magic meditations with Papa Bear. The next verse was "Mind is empty." Right now, her mind felt more foggy than empty. Cinderwan composed herself.

The ashes were warm. Cinderwan stroked them with her hand. As she did, a rounded object became visible near the surface. She dusted it off. It was a turquoise egg with a golden zero on its side. "Niner," she said, smiling and patting the egg.

"Yes," said Mama Bear. "The Phoenix. Well, Zero. And technically the egg is a proto-phoenix. Our Phoenix will show up after a while."

It was a turquoise egg with a golden zero on its side.

Cinderwan lifted the egg gently and carried it to a blanket. Jorgan watched. He went to fetch another blanket.

Cinderwan's hands were dusty. She brushed them together. Then on impulse she snapped her finger. A flame shot up from her thumb. She smiled and said, "So it wasn't just a dream."

Mama Bear smiled. "As the prophecy predicted," she said. "You are ready to be trained in the Fire Element. There has been a healing. Pele will explain."

She gently blew out the flame from Cinderwan's raised thumb.

"Best not show off that talent," she said to Cinderwan. "But it can come in handy for lighting the oven when you are baking pies."

Cinderwan noticed that Mama Bear was crying and laughing quietly.

11 Pele

ama Bear guided Cinderwan down a steep path from the peak. They were on a cliff above the sea. A sea breeze cleared the sulfurous fumes. The air became fresh and salty. Hot lava steamed as it touched the water. It cooled to become rock.

"The way of the fire is bright and hot," sang Cinderwan.

Pele rose from the sea and gazed at Cinderella.

"The walk is outside, but the journey is not," continued Mama Bear. "The Fire Ballad is quite literal. It is a calling to come to Pele for training. This is where the island grows, where fire creates land. I will leave you now to meet with Pele. I will return in an hour or so."

Mama Bear hugged Cinderwan. Cinderwan hugged her back. She stood near a bench and watched the hot lava flowing into the sea.

Suddenly the lava pooled up and rose from the sea. A woman's figure formed. It was Pele, gazing directly at Cinderwan.

Pele spoke. "Fire powers creation," she said. "Tell me, Cinderwan. How does the 'created' know what form to take?"

Cinderwan bowed. "Earth Mother, Pele," she said, remembering Mama Bear's instructions about the proper form of address. Pele was asking her about creation and the energies of creation.

Cinderwan spoke again. "May I consider this out loud?" she asked.

Pele nodded. "There is no hurry, Cinderwan."

"Crystals form as crystals. Rock forms as rock. Metal forms as metal. Everything forms according to its nature."

Pele was quiet for a while. Then she asked, "But how can each thing know its nature?"

Cinderwan puzzled.

"I am not sure," she said.

"Think of your dream," suggested the lava woman. "What does it tell you?"

"You know my dream?" asked Cinderwan.

Pele smiled, "First comes the dream. Then comes the creation."

Cinderwan remembered her dream about falling into the volcano before the Phoenix burned on his pyre. "In my dream, I *remembered* an event from my childhood. Perhaps we have to *remember* who we are."

"Good," Pele said, "But before a thing is created it is formless. If we are formless, how can we dream? How can we remember?"

Cinderwan thought more about her dream. "I 'remembered' that I could not sing. Then I saw that my stepsisters had misled me long ago in order to defeat me. I spent many sad years without singing! My belief was an illusion."

"So, what takes you beyond that?" asked Pele.

"The Phoenix told me to sing my song. I had to reclaim my voice," answered Cinderwan.

"Yes," said Pele. "Your old memory misled you. You needed to sing from your heart. This dream is perfect for the Phoenix!"

Cinderwan began to see the mystery more clearly. She faced Pele. "May I ask a question?"

Pele smiled. "There will be many questions, Cinderwan. I will answer, according to your readiness."

Cinderwan continued. "Thank you. I was told that the Phoenix has been here since the beginning. What beginning? The beginning of the Elders? Could it mean the beginning of the world? I do not understand this."

Pele answered, "You are pursuing an important line of inquiry for your destiny. You will learn to sharpen your questions to address what matters most. I will ask you a question that may help."

Pele continued. "Think of the ocean and waves. How is the Phoenix like a wave?"

Cinderwan thought for a moment. "A wave comes and then the next wave comes. Each wave forms, rises, and then disappears."

She continued, "The Phoenix forms when it hatches from its egg. Then it grows and has a life. After a while, it burns on its pyre and returns to being an egg."

Pele nodded. "Go on," she encouraged.

Cinderwan continued. "So, each wave is like a Phoenix. There is wave #1, wave #2, and wave #3 just as there is Phoenix #1, Phoenix #2, and Phoenix #3. So, when I ask you about the age of a Phoenix, do I mean a particular wave, or the 'first wave' if there is such a thing? I did not understand what question to ask."

Pele smiled. "Here is another question for you. What is the relationship between water, air, and sky?"

Cinderwan smiled. "I do love blue! The question makes me feel silly. Well, when there is a great wind, it stirs up many waves."

Pele interrupted her. "Perhaps a traditional koan will guide you."

> What is the pattern
> Of water on air?
> Does air shape the water?
> Of water the air?

"When the young Phoenix needs to know something, the Scholar opens the book."

Cinderwan opened her mouth to answer quickly, and then stopped herself. She started again and hesitated. Finally, she spoke, "Water must

51

shape the air. It is heavier, more liquid than gas." She paused to think. "But air also stirs up the water."

Cinderwan turned to Pele. "Are you suggesting that air and water shape each other? Are you saying that neither came first, neither the Phoenix nor the world?"

Pele smiled. "Your investigation moves forward," she said enigmatically.

"When the young Phoenix needs to remember his previous lives," asked Pele. "How will he remember his true nature?"

"The Scholar carries a big book of songs," suggested Cinderwan. "He carries it on this journey. Perhaps the songs hint at important memories from the Phoenix's previous lives. Does the Phoenix recognize the truth in the songs and then regain parts of his memories when he hears them?"

"Your intuition serves you well," said Pele. "There has been a lot of squeaking and chirping on parts of the island," she laughed.

"The Phoenix's songs!" said Cinderwan. "But how do they know what part of the book to read?"

"It is the nature of his mind," answered Pele. "The young Phoenix's mind is prepared to learn. Whenever there is something he needs to know, the Scholar opens the book. The book inspires and instructs him."

Cinderwan was intrigued. "So as the Phoenix grows, he regains his memory. Oh, wow! May we talk more?"

"We have much to discuss, Cinderwan."

"I have so many questions," continued Cinderwan. "Why am I being trained in Five Elements? What is my connection to the Phoenix? Who were all those other strange people in the dream? I sense that these questions and my dream are not just about my training in Fire, and they are more than my wild imagination."

Pele smiled. "Welcome to your journey, Cinderwan. Your training has begun."

The lava stopped flowing. The air became still. The waves became motionless on the ocean. Pele had stopped time around them.

The Pele appeared at human scale facing Cinderwan. She took Cinderwan's hand. "You need to understand the Fire Magic in your core. Its power is enormous, and there is great responsibility when using it. It can be overwhelming. Fire can be used to create or destroy."

"You will learn many songs. You will also create songs that have never been sung before. You will sing songs of creation and destruction. Much will depend on you."

As they walked, the land shifted around them to show the beauty of Hawaii in the coming years. Pele was shifting time. The rocks would turn into a lush paradise. The songs of future Hawaii were about a tropical island.

Pele trained Cinderwan for a year. Cinderwan was tested and trained and trained and tested.

An hour after she left, Mama Bear returned. She found Cinderwan sitting on the bench waiting for her. Cinderwan looked rested and clean and wore a different outfit. She radiated strength and confidence.

"How are you?" began Mama Bear.

Cinderwan sighed. "I do not completely know what I am being prepared for," she began. "Or what I am becoming." She smiled. "Still, I feel stronger!"

Mama Bear was thoughtful. "How long were you with Pele?" she asked.

"It was a moment. It was an hour. It was a year," answered Cinderwan.

Pele took human scale and walked with Cinderwan.

"I see the light in you, Mama Bear of the Fire Element," sang Cinderwan melodiously.

"I see the light in you," sang Mama Bear back. "Cinderwan of the Earth Element *and* Cinderwan of the Fire Element."

Mama Bear closed her eyes for a moment and then looked deeply at Cinderwan. Cinderwan radiated the light of the Fire Element. Power could be used to create or destroy. There would be temptation.

They hugged and walked along the path to join the others.

12 Grimmicus Ponders the Ordinary

The confusion in the planning for a Sol #3 expedition is a case in point. Understanding what is ordinary or extraordinary depends on a point of view. Thinking like a native requires recognizing and setting aside the assumptions of your own culture. *Grimmicus, A Biography, Stuarticus Cardicus.*

oubt is the issue," announced Smithicus #2.

"Doubt is the issue."

Smithicus #2 added, "We *should* mount a full-scale expedition to Sol #3 backed with battle-bots. There may be a force on Sol #3 preparing to invade Zorcon and turn our robots against us. However, the cost for a full-scale invasion mission would be high. The accountants are not convinced that there is a real danger. Smithicus #1 offered a different expedition proposal where Oversight spy agents would pose as anthropologists. An expedition in force could come later if needed.

Grimmicus was amused by the gaps in Oversight's understanding of the methods of planetary anthropology. Natives are unaware of planetary anthropologists. Planetary anthropologists go undercover. They pose as natives, not as anthropologists.

"But you can't deny that it is *extraordinary* that a home appliance was reprogrammed," said Smithicus #2.

"But only one appliance was effected, and it happened during a massive power outage," replied Smithicus #1. "Perhaps there was a glitch. In the grand scheme of things, that might make the misbehaving android rather *ordinary*."

"You must already have orbiting surveillance probes."

The two Smiths, as Grimmicus called the Oversight agents, were in his conference room again. Funding for an expedition to Sol #3 was being discussed. The discussion seemed more like a qualifying exam for students than a funding discussion. The Smiths were at least marginally trained in logic.

"Surely you already have surveillance of Sol #3 from orbiting probes," remarked Grimmicus. "If you had found unexplained energy use, that evidence would be compelling for the accountants."

The two agents looked at each other. "That information is classified," said Smithicus #1.

Grimmicus knew at once that this topic had been thoroughly discussed. There were orbiting surveillance satellites. They had found no evidence of energy usage. He smiled but said nothing while he considered what he was learning.

"Effective shielding of power use would be *extraordinary*," Grimmicus offered cautiously.

"Especially if it did not significantly alter system entropy," added Smithicus #2.

Smithicus #1 glared at Smithicus #2. That comment came too close to revealing strategic capabilities. He sighed. "Without evidence, the simplest interpretation is that there *is* nothing there. That makes it *ordinary*."

Smithicus #1 glared at Smithicus #2.

Grimmicus was getting into the debating rhythm now. He offered, "There are no other appliances on Sol #3 to disrupt. But there is other Zorcon technology. One might check for tampering of GottMothercus' transputer."

The agents looked at each other again. Grimmicus recognized a "tell." As field agents, they should learn to hide their thinking better. Their investigation had revealed no tampering with her "wand."

Grimmicus continued his questions. "Your video from the wand's memory showed that 'Charley' was not destroyed. If the alleged space-travelling aliens had tampered with the wand, they would be motivated to erase all data about Charley. You would have your evidence and mission funding would not be in question. Therefore, they did not tamper," he concluded.

"Classified," said Smithicus #1, who was gaining a greater appreciation for Grimmicus. The professor was dangerous. His powers of deduction put him in a special league. "This conversation is now classified on a need-to-know basis. You know the rules?"

Grimmicus nodded. Now perhaps he would learn something.

"No tampering detected," said Smithicus #2, who had been burning to share what he knew.

"*Extraordinary*," said Grimmicus.

"*Ordinary*," said Smithicus #2. "Perhaps the aliens are careless. They may not know that we can tap into the wand."

"But the *reputed* aliens supposedly had the capability to take over an appliance," said Grimmicus, shifting his argument. "That would require understanding our technology very deeply. Perhaps there are aliens, but they don't care if we know about them. They would be very confident, indeed."

"Extraordinary!"

"The simplest interpretation is that there are no dangerous aliens," said Smithicus #1. "Ordinary."

"*Extraordinary!*" sighed Grimmicus, thinking about beauty of the logical puzzle.

"Not funny," said Smithicus #1, smiling anyway.

"What about evidence that the natives are showing *extraordinary* capabilities or using high technology?" asked Grimmicus.

"A party of natives is flying half-way around the world now," answered Smithicus #2.

"Extraordinary!" exclaimed Grimmicus, feeling surprised. "With more flying vehicles like the Santa sled?"

"No. On the backs of flying creatures, called 'dragons,'" said Smithicus #1.

"No technology. So, it's *ordinary*," continued Smithicus #1.

"They take this flight every six months, apparently as part of a student exchange program," he continued.

"*Extraordinary*," said Grimmicus.

"It doesn't signal any cautionary alerts for us. They fly, but so do birds. They do not have space flight or interstellar capability. So, it's *ordinary*," commented Smithicus #1.

"The appliance is being trained in their school system," offered Smithicus #1.

"A logical way to train him," said Grimmicus, thinking of Zorcon University.

"A school for robots," joked Smithicus #2. "*Extraordinary!*"

"Knock it off," said Smithicus #1. "We have found nothing actionable. We need to test our hypothesis."

"We could introduce a second appliance. Then we could wait to see what happens," said Grimmicus, thinking about setting a trap to catch the alleged aliens.

Smithicus #2 looked at Smithicus #1. They smiled. Grimmicus wondered whether they had already thought of this. Perhaps the entire conversation was intended to lead *him* to make that suggestion. He may have underestimated the two Smiths.

Then Grimmicus smiled, "I would be happy to suggest this to Marie. Creating a suitable appliance would not be difficult. Marie does not like to do housework."

"Marie might be hesitant to make another appliance."

Inwardly, however, he wondered. Marie was embarrassed by what had happened to Charley. She might be hesitant to make another appliance.

About the Author

Mark Stefik and his wife, Barbara Stefik, live in northern California. Mark is a computer scientist and inventor. Barbara is a transpersonal psychologist and researcher. They illustrate the stories together.

They can be contacted through their website at

www.PortolaPublishing.com

Made in the USA
Middletown, DE
30 April 2021

38801678R00042